Taking Flight

se i
car
te

D0656244

White Wolves Series Consultant: Sue Ellis,
Centre for Literacy in Primary Education

This book can be used in the White Wolves Guided Reading programme
with children who need a lot of support with reading at Year 4 level

Reprinted 2008
First published 2006 by
A & C Black Publishers Ltd
38 Soho Square, London, W1D 3HB

www.acblack.com

Text copyright © 2006 Julia Green
Illustrations copyright © 2006 Jane Cope

The rights of Julia Green and Jane Cope to be identified
as author and illustrator of this work respectively have been
asserted by them in accordance with the Copyrights,
Designs and Patents Act 1988.

ISBN 978-0-7136-7594-8

A CIP catalogue for this book is available from the British Library.

This book is produced using paper that is made from wood grown in
managed, sustainable forests. It is natural, renewable and recyclable.
The logging and manufacturing processes conform to the
environmental rgeulations of the country of origin.

Printed and bound in Great Britain by Cox and Wyman Ltd.

Taking Flight

Julia Green

Illustrated by Jane Cope

A & C Black • London

Contents

Chapter One

Tick. Tick. The big hand on the
clock clicks round to three. At last!
Luke pushes back his chair and
lets out a big sigh. He doesn't
mean it to make
a noise, but it
does. His
teacher
frowns.

7

"Thanks for the reminder, Luke. OK, everyone. Time to go home. Put everything away in your drawers, please. And don't forget tonight's homework. I want each of you to prepare a short talk about something that interests you, for tomorrow. Off you go."

The playground is full of
people: mums and dads and
carers and big sisters and brothers,
all waiting to collect children from
St Giles' Primary School.

Luke pushes past them. He
goes home by himself.

Well, not home, exactly. Luke goes to Grandad's house, which is twelve minutes fifty seconds' walk away from the school.

It's his favourite place ever. For a start, Grandad is there. Grandad lets Luke make pancakes for tea (and supper and breakfast).

He doesn't ask questions like *what did you learn at school today?* or *what homework have you got tonight?* He doesn't moan about Luke's muddy shoes, or tell him to turn the TV off. There are interesting things to look at on the shelves: fossils, and a small brass telescope, and a compass.

And then there's the garden. It's long and thin, with trees you can climb and grass you can run on.

At the bottom of the garden are the sheds. One is empty apart from a few tools. It's the perfect place for sitting in when you want to be quiet and think. It smells of hay. The other shed is the pigeon loft.

Luke pushes the door open. It's like stepping into another world.

The air is full of the sound of soft bird calls: *crrroo, crooo*. It makes Luke think of cats purring. Feathers float in the warm air. The birds peck at the seed in their boxes and preen their feathers. Their eyes are beady bright. They watch Luke. They know him. They're not scared.

Luke talks to them. He tells them secrets, sometimes – how he doesn't like school. Today, he tells them about football.

"I'm useless at it. I don't even like it, really, but everybody else does. So that makes me different."

The pigeons coo back. One tries to peck his finger when he holds his hand against the wire mesh. It tickles. He laughs.

Close up, you can see all different colours in their feathers. Green, and purple, and pink and silver.

Luke hears Grandad coming slowly down the garden. These days, he walks with a stick.

"Shall we let them out for a fly around?" Grandad asks.

Luke nods. Together, they watch the birds hop onto the edge of the cage as each door is opened. Suddenly they all take flight, off and up into the blue, summer sky. Their wings flash like silver in the sunlight as they wheel round, a silver arc above the houses and gardens and streets.

"Let's have our tea outside today," Grandad says.

They are still there when the pigeons come back to roost. They hear the swish of wings as the birds circle over the plum tree.

Mum tuts at Grandad when she comes to collect Luke on her way home from work. "You'll catch cold," she says. "The garden's all in shadow, now."

In the car, she tells Luke he ought to help Grandad in the house more.

"Didn't you see the piles of dirty dishes in the sink?" she asks.

"And dust everywhere. He's getting old. He shouldn't really be living by himself."

Luke knows Grandad wouldn't dream of living anywhere else.

"Finished your homework, I hope," Mum says, like it's a question.

Luke nods. He hasn't, of course. He's forgotten all about it, on purpose. He doesn't want to give a talk. He hates talking in front of the whole class.

He thinks about it again at bedtime. He stays awake, worrying. He listens to the owls outside his window.

Even in a town there are owls. Perhaps he could do his talk about Grandad's pigeons, he thinks, just before he falls asleep.

Chapter Two

"I don't feel well," Luke tells Mum at breakfast.

"What's wrong?" she says.

"I feel sick."

"Well, we'll just have to hope you don't get any worse," she says. "I've got a busy day. I can't stay at home. I'm sorry, Luke."

"I could stay with Grandad," Luke says, hopefully.

"No," Mum says. "Grandad needs time to rest. It's enough for him having you after school every day."

"He *likes* having me," Luke says. "He says it's the highlight of his day!"

But Mum is already getting the car keys and her coat.

Most of Luke's class are in the middle of a football game in the playground when he arrives at the gate. He stands next to Mira and watches Sam and Marek dribbling the ball like professionals. Marek scores a goal.

"What are you doing for your talk?" Mira asks him.

Luke shrugs. "Nothing," he says. "I forgot."

They start doing the talks after lunch. Luke feels sicker and sicker. What is he going to do? Mira talks about going to India for her aunty's wedding. She shows the class the sequinned sari she wore. Marek talks about the Junior League – he's goalie. Joe's talk is about the newts he has in his garden pond. The newts have little hands.

Luke wonders about having a pond in Grandad's garden, with newts. The whole class clap when each person finishes. It's not so bad, after all, Luke thinks. It's fun listening to everyone.

Luke watches the clock. *Tick. Tick.* Nearly there. *Tick Tick.* Home time!

"I'm sorry, children," Mrs Hill says. "We'll have to save the last four talks for tomorrow."

YES! Luke thinks. Now he's got time to get a really good talk ready. He imagines everyone listening and clapping.

He tells Grandad what he's decided. "Tomorrow I'm giving a talk about your pigeons."

"Good lad," Grandad says. "Maple syrup or lemon and sugar for your pancakes?"

Luke has both. So does
Grandad. Luke remembers to help
do the washing-up. Grandad has a
sleep in the deckchair. He sleeps for
ages, so Luke feeds the pigeons and
lets them out for their fly around.

"I'm going to tell everyone at
school about you tomorrow," he
tells them as they perch on the
cage edge, ready
for takeoff.

They tip their heads and look
at him with their beady eyes.
The pigeons fly off with a swoop
of wings. Two feathers flutter
down. Luke picks them up. He can
take them in to show his class.

He watches the birds spiral
above the gardens in bigger and
bigger circles, and then veer off over
the street. Maybe they are flying
over the school. Perhaps Grandad
would let them out when he did
his talk, so everyone could see.

Luke goes over to ask him.
But Grandad looks strange. His
face is grey. He's shivering.

"Give us a
hand in, lad,"
Grandad says.

Luke makes
him a cup of tea
but he doesn't
drink it.

"I think we'd better get your
mum here," Grandad says. Luke
phones her mobile.

"I'm on my way," she says.
"Keep him warm. Call the doctor
if he gets worse."

Luke brings a blanket downstairs and tucks it round Grandad. He sits by him. Grandad strokes his hand. They watch the TV till Mum arrives.

She phones the doctor. The doctor says they need to get an ambulance. Grandad gets bundled into the ambulance. Mum and Luke follow in the car.

At the hospital, Luke has to wait on a chair in a corridor for ages. He suddenly remembers the pigeons. They will need shutting back in their cages safe for the night. He tells Mum when she comes back.

"Grandad needs to stay in hospital tonight," she says. "Come and see him before we go."

Grandad is lying in a bed. The white sheets make his face look grey. Luke thinks Grandad looks older and a bit sad.

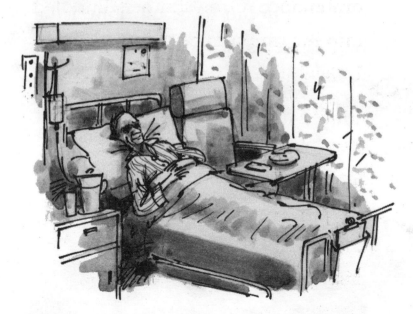

"Take care of them pigeons for me, lad," Grandad says.

"I will, Grandad. I'll feed them till you're safe back home."

When Luke turns round to wave from the doorway, Grandad has already closed his eyes.

"He's going to be all right, isn't he?" Luke asks.

"He's in the best place right now," Mum says.

Chapter Three

Luke's hands are shaking as he stands in front of his class.

"Right," Mrs Hill says. "What are you going to tell us about, Luke?"

"Pigeons," Luke says. His voice comes out too soft, and a bit squeaky. Someone giggles.

Mrs Hill frowns. "Quiet, everyone," she says. "Speak up, Luke."

Once he's got going it isn't so
bad. He tells the class about the
pigeon loft, and
how to put seed
in the hopper,
and fill the
water trough.
He makes the
sound of a
happy pigeon: *crrroo crooo.*

"Their feathers are beautiful,
if you look properly," Luke says.
"Pink and turquoise and green,
not just grey like people think."
He passes round the two feathers
for everyone to stroke.

"Best of all is when the pigeons fly off, in a great circle, and their wings flash silver in the sunlight as they turn."

"Why don't they just fly away?" Mira asks.

"Because they know where they're fed, see?" Luke says.

"They're homers, and you can train them."

"Have they got names?" Joe says.

"Yes. Each one's different, see? There's Silver, with his silvery head, and Bossy, who's the lead bird, and Queenie, because of the way she walks..."

Luke's forgotten that he was scared about talking in front of everyone. It's easy. Everyone's listening, and asking questions.

Mrs Hill gives him a big smile. "Well done, Luke!" she says. "We need to stop now, but that was fascinating. Thank you."

Everyone claps.

"You were brilliant," Mira says at the end of the day.

Luke blushes.

"Can I come and see them pigeons?" Joe asks.

"When my Grandad's better," Luke says.

Mum finishes work early so she can collect Luke from school and they can both go to the hospital.

"Had a good day?" Mum asks.

"Yes," Luke says. He's surprised. It really was a good day. His talk was pretty cool.

They tiptoe through the door into the ward. Grandad seems to be sleeping. Mum sits in the chair next to the bed, and Luke stands next to her. Grandad's breathing sounds funny. Mum strokes Grandad's hand. He opens his eyes. He doesn't recognise them at first. He thinks Luke is someone else.

"Speak to him, Luke," Mum says.

"I did my talk about your pigeons today," Luke says. "Everyone liked it."

"Good lad," Grandad says. "How are my beauties?"

"They're missing you," Luke says. "I fed them this morning on the way to school. I'll let them out, later."

"Good lad." Grandad closes his eyes again.

"He's very tired," Mum says. "We better not stay too long.'

"Tired," Grandad echoes. "Tired out."

Mum drives back via Grandad's so Luke can look after the pigeons. "I'll do a spot of cleaning while you let them out," she says.

Luke gets the key and goes down the garden. The pigeons are crowding against the wire in their cages in the shed, jostling for space at the front, cooing and pecking at the empty seed hoppers.

"It's all right," Luke tells them. "I'm looking after you now."

As he unlatches each cage, the birds push and shove their way onto the edge and then take off in sudden flight. Luke watches each single bird become part of the whole, so that they fly together in a silvery wave, high over the rooftops and away towards the park.

Luke cleans out the cages with the special brush Grandad uses. He refills the feed and water. Then he sweeps out the shed and makes everything tidy. All the time he imagines Grandad is there, watching him.

Mum wanders down the garden. "Tea's ready," she says. "We can have it here, today."

"Grandad's a very sick man," she tells Luke, as they eat.

"I know," Luke says. "I can see that. He's not going to get better, is he?"

"Probably not," Mum says, and a tear trickles down her cheek.

Luke holds her hand. He doesn't want to cry, but he can't help it.

Chapter Four

On Saturday, Mum drives Luke
round to Grandad's house as
usual so he can look after the
pigeons. She has cleaned the whole
house by now, top to bottom. She
picks flowers to go
in the blue china
jug on the kitchen
table. Luke makes
pancakes for them
both for breakfast.

"I wish Grandad were here," he says.

"Me too," Mum says.

"Couldn't we bring him home and look after him?"

Mum sighs. "It would be nicer for him," she says.

Luke talks to the pigeons while he gives them some corn. "What do you think? Grandad might get better if he came back home, don't you think?"

"*Croo, croo*," they say.

Luke reckons that means yes.

When they get to the hospital ward, Luke and Mum have a shock. Grandad isn't there.

A nurse walks over. Her shoes make a squeaky sound on the floor. "Mrs Taylor?" she says.

"Yes?" Mum says. "Where's my dad?" Her voice sounds panicky. Luke feels his heart beating faster, too.

"We've moved him," the nurse says, "to his own room, to give him a bit of peace and quiet." The nurse looks at Luke, and then at Mum. "Can I have a private word?" she says.

Luke watches them talking together. He feels sad and heavy inside.

He knows where the single rooms are. He goes to find Grandad by himself.

Grandad doesn't look like
Grandad any more. His eyes are
sunken and dull. His skin seems
paper thin, and his bony hand on
the sheet is curved like a claw.

"Luke?" Grandad whispers.
"Thank goodness you've come."
A tear rolls down one of his
papery cheeks.

"What is it, Grandad?" Luke touches his hand, even though he feels scared.

"Take me home," Grandad whispers. "Please."

Mum arrives at the door. She puts sweet peas she's brought from the garden close to Grandad's face so he can smell them. For a second, something  like a smile hovers on his lips.

"We've got to take Grandad home," Luke says.

"Yes," Mum says. "I've already told the nurse that's what we're going to do."

Luke and Mum go first, to get everything ready, and then an ambulance brings Grandad. The ambulance men carry Grandad inside. They tuck him into bed on the sofa in the front room, so he doesn't have to go upstairs.

Mum goes back to the flat to fetch clothes for her and Luke.

"We need to move in here for a while to take care of Grandad," she explains.

Luke hugs her. "Good. We should have done that ages ago," he says.

Mum laughs. "Grandad wouldn't have let us! He loved being on his own, in his own place, doing exactly what he wanted. Just him, and those blessed pigeons, of course!"

From his sofa bed, Grandad can glimpse a square of sky and when Luke lets the pigeons out for a fly around, he can hear the beating of their wings.

He smiles, weakly. "That's better," he says.

He sleeps most of the time.
Luke understands that Grandad is
tired out. Tired of living, now.

"I've had a good life," Grandad
says. "Time to go, soon."

It makes Luke feel very sad.
Sunday evening, Luke carries

Queenie and Silver into the house,
so Grandad can say goodbye to
his favourite pigeons. The birds
nestle on
Grandad's
knees,
on the
blanket,
and he
smoothes their
feathers with his hand.

"Time for me to take flight,"
he whispers to them.

Chapter Five

Luke wakes up in the night. It must be nearly dawn, because the window is pale grey instead of black. He hears Mum's feet on the stairs. Then he hears her talking to someone on the phone.

Luke climbs out of bed and goes onto the landing. There's a lamp on downstairs. Mum comes out of the front room. She looks up.

"He's gone," she says softly.
"Grandad's died.'

They sit on the stairs, and cry
together. When Luke goes back to
bed, he lies there remembering all
the happy times he's had with
Grandad.

He dreams about Grandad
and the pigeons. The pigeons
are carrying Grandad with them
as they circle and spiral into the
blue sky.

When Luke wakes up, he knows
Grandad is happy, and safe,
wherever he is now.

After the funeral is over, Luke goes back to school.

"We missed you," Mira says.

"Want to play football?" Marek and Sam ask, at lunchtime.

"No, thanks," Luke says, but he's pleased they asked him all the same.

He sits with Joe under the tree in the playground.

"The pigeons are mine now," Luke tells Joe. "And we've moved into my grandad's house, so I've got a garden, too. We might make a pond."

"I'll help you," Joe says. "And in the spring, I'll give you some of my newt spawn."

"You can come and meet my pigeons, if you like," Luke says.

"Tomorrow?"

"OK," Luke smiles.

Luke walks home from school.
It takes him exactly twelve minutes
and fifty seconds. He goes straight
to the pigeon loft. His pigeons are
waiting for him.

"All right, steady on," he tells them as they push and jostle at the wire. As he unlocks each cage the pigeons hop onto the edge and spread their wings for flight.

Luke watches them. Their silver wings flash in the sunlight as they spiral in the blue sky.

Luke remembers his dream. "Happy flight, Grandad," he whispers. He feels sure Grandad is still watching him, somehow.

Mum's car pulls up. She calls from the gate. "Luke? I'm home."

"Coming," he says. "I'll make us pancakes for tea."

About the Author

Julia Green writes mainly for young adults. *Blue Moon*, *Baby Blue* and *Hunter's Heart* are all published by Puffin. She lives in Bath with her two teenage children, and lectures in creative writing at Bath Spa University. She is programme leader for the MA in Writing for Young People. She also runs writing workshops for young people and adults.

Other White Wolves that raise issues...

J. Alexander

Carly is being teased and excluded
from the group of girls who were
once her best friends. She tries to put
a brave face on it, but it's clear she
has 'lost her fizz'. Then Carly finds
a stray dog that needs a loving home
and all at once life starts looking
very different...

Finding Fizz is a story about bullying
and being 'one of the gang'.

ISBN: 978-0-7136-7625-9   £4.99

Other White Wolves that raise issues...

Nothing But Trouble

Alan MacDonald

It's a tough job for Paul being Jago's 'buddy' at school. The new boy comes from a family of travellers and he doesn't say much or seem interested in making friends. Then Paul discovers Jago has a secret and a special bond develops between the two boys, but how long can it last?

Nothing But Trouble is a story about prejudice and not fitting in.

ISBN: 978-0-7136-7679-2   £4.99

Year 4